Winter in Sokcho

Copyright © 2016 by Elisa Shua Dusapin
Translation copyright © 2020 by Aneesa Abbas Higgins
First UK edition from Daunt Books, 2020

First edition, 2021
All rights reserved

Library of Congress Cataloging-in-Publication Data: Available.
ISBN-13: 978-1-948830-41-6 | ISBN-10: 1-948830-41-8

*This project is supported in part by an award from the New York State Council on the Arts
with the support of Governor Andrew M. Cuomo and the New York State Legislature.*

Printed on acid-free paper in the United States of America.

Cover Design by Luke Bird

Open Letter is the University of Rochester's nonprofit, literary translation press:
Dewey Hall 1-219, Box 278968, Rochester, NY 14627

www.openletterbooks.org

Winter in Sokcho

ELISA SHUA DUSAPIN

Translated by Aneesa Abbas Higgins

OPEN LETTER
LITERARY TRANSLATIONS FROM THE UNIVERSITY OF ROCHESTER

HE ARRIVED bundled up in a woolen coat.

He put his suitcase down at my feet and pulled off his hat. Western face. Dark eyes. Hair combed to one side. He looked straight through me, without seeing me. Somewhat impatiently, he asked me in English if he could stay for a few days while he looked around for something else. I gave him a registration form to fill in. He handed me his passport so I could do it for him. Yan Kerrand, 1968, from Granville. A Frenchman. He seemed younger than in the photo, his cheeks less hollow. I held out my pencil for him to sign and he took a pen from his coat. While I was checking him in, he pulled off his gloves, placed them on the counter, inspected the dust, the cat figurine on the wall above the computer. I felt compelled, for the first time since I'd started at the guest house, to make excuses for myself. I wasn't responsible for the run-down state of the place. I'd only been working there a month.

There were two buildings. In the main building, the reception, kitchen and visitors' lounge downstairs, and a hallway lined with guest rooms. Another hallway with more guest rooms upstairs. Orange and green corridors, lit by bluish light bulbs. Old Park hadn't moved on from the days after the war, when guests were lured like squid to their nets, dazzled by strings of blinking lights. From the boiler room, on clear days, I could see the beach stretching all the way to the Ulsan mountains that swelled on the horizon. The second building was around the back of the first one, down a long alleyway. A traditional house on stilts, restored to make the most of its two rooms with their heated floors and paper dividing walls. An internal courtyard with a frozen fountain and a bare chestnut tree. There was no mention of Old Park's in the guidebooks. People washed up there by chance, when they'd had too much to drink or missed the last bus home.

The computer froze. I left it to recover while I went over the information for guests with the Frenchman. It was usually Old Park's job to do this but he wasn't there that day. Breakfast from 5 A.M. to 10, in the kitchen next to the reception, through the sliding glass door. No charge for toast, butter, jam, coffee, tea, orange juice, and milk. Fruit and yogurt extra, put a thousand won in the basket on top of the toaster. Items to be washed should be left in the machine at the end of the corridor on the ground floor, I'd take care of the laundry. Wi-Fi password: ilovesokcho, all one word, no capitals. Convenience store open twenty-four hours a day, fifty meters down the road. Bus stop on the left just past the shop. Seoraksan National Park, one hour away, open all day until sunset. A good pair of boots recommended, for the snow. He should bear in mind that Sokcho was a seaside resort, I added. There wasn't much to do in the winter.

Guests were few and far between at that time of year. A Japanese climber, and a girl about my age, seeking refuge from the capital while she recovered from plastic surgery to her face. She'd been at the guest house for about two weeks, her boyfriend had just joined her for ten days. I'd put all three of them in the main house. Business had been slow since the death of Park's wife the previous year.

Park had closed up the upstairs bedrooms. When you included my room and Park's, all the rooms were taken. The Frenchman could sleep in the other building.

It was dark. We set off down the narrow alleyway past Mother Kim's stall. Her pork balls gave off an aroma of garlic and drains that lingered in the mouth all the way down the street. Ice cracked beneath our feet. Pallid neon lights. We crossed a second alleyway and came to the front porch.

Kerrand slid the door open. Pink paint, plastic faux baroque mirror, desk, purple bedspread. His head brushed the ceiling, from wall to bed was no more than two steps for him. I'd given him the smallest room in the building, to save on cleaning. The communal bathroom was across the courtyard, but he wouldn't get wet, there was a covered walkway all around the house. It didn't bother him anyway. He examined the stains on the wallpaper, put down his suitcase, handed me five thousand won. I tried to refuse it but he insisted, wearily.

On my way back to reception, I took a detour through the fish market to pick up the leftovers my mother had put aside for me. I walked down the aisles to stand number forty-two, ignoring the looks people gave me as I passed. My French origins were still a source of gossip even though it was twenty-three years since my father had seduced my mother and then vanished without a trace.

My mother, wearing too much makeup as usual, handed me a bag of baby octopus:

"That's all there is right now. Have you got any bean paste left?"

"Yes."

"I'll give you some."

"No need, I still have some."

"Why don't you use it?"

"I do!"

Her rubber gloves made a sucking noise as she pulled them on and looked at me suspiciously. I'd lost weight. Old Park didn't give me enough time to eat, she'd have a word with him. I told her not to. I'd been consuming vast amounts of toast and milky coffee every morning ever since I'd started working there, I said, I couldn't possibly have lost weight. Old Park had taken a while to get used to my cooking but he didn't interfere. The kitchen was my domain.

The octopus were tiny, ten or so to a handful. I sorted through them, browned them with shallots, soy sauce, sugar, and diluted bean paste. I reduced the heat to stop them getting too dry. When the sauce had thickened, I added some sesame and *tteok*, slices of small sticky rice balls. Then I started to chop the carrots. Reflected in the blade of the knife, their grooved surface blended weirdly with the flesh of my fingers.

I felt a chill as a draft blew through the kitchen. Turning around I saw Kerrand come in. He wanted a glass of water. He watched me work while he drank it, staring hard as if he were trying to make sense of the image in front of him. I lost concentration and nicked the palm of my hand. Blood welled onto the carrots, hardening to form a brownish crust. Kerrand took a handkerchief from his pocket. He stood close to me and held it to the wound.

"You should be more careful."

"I didn't do it on purpose."

"Just as well."

He smiled, pressing his hand against mine. I broke away, feeling uneasy. He nodded toward the pan.

"Is that for this evening?"

"Yes, seven o'clock, in the next room."

"You're bleeding."

Irony, statement of fact, distaste. I couldn't read the tone of his voice. And besides, he'd already left.

At dinner, there was no sign of him.

MY MOTHER WAS squatting in the kitchen, her chin pressed to her neck, arms plunged into a bucket. She was mixing fish liver, leeks, and sweet potato noodles to make the stuffing for the squid. Her *soondae* were known to be the best in Sokcho.

"Watch me work the mixture. See how I spread the stuffing evenly."

I wasn't really listening. Liquid was spurting out from the bucket, pooling around our boots and running toward the drain in the middle of the room. My mother lived at the port, above the loading bays, in one of the apartments reserved for fishmongers. Noisy. Cheap. My childhood home. I went to see her on Sunday evenings and stayed over until Monday, my day off. She'd been finding it difficult sleeping alone since I'd moved out.

Handing me a squid to stuff, she placed her liver-stained gloves on my hips and sighed:

"So young and pretty, and still not married . . ."

"Jun-oh has to find a job first. We've got plenty of time."

"People always think they have time."

"I'm only twenty-four."

"Exactly."

I promised her we'd get engaged officially, in a few months' time. Reassured, my mother went back to her task.

That night, between the damp sheets, crushed by the weight of her head on my stomach, I felt her chest rising and falling as she slept. I'd gotten used to sleeping alone in the guest house. Her snoring kept me awake. I counted the drops of saliva leaking out one by one from her parted lips and onto my skin.

THE NEXT DAY I went for a walk on the beach that ran the length of the town. I loved this coastline, scarred as it was by the line of electrified barbed wire fencing along the shore. The border with North Korea was barely sixty kilometers away. A windblown figure stood out against the building works in the harbor. The name in the passport flashed through my mind. Yan Kerrand, walking toward me. A dog sprang up from a pile of nets and began to follow him, sniffing at his trousers. One of the workers called the dog back. Kerrand stopped to stroke it, said something that sounded like "that's okay," but the man put the dog back on its lead, and Kerrand carried on walking toward me.

He drew level with me and I fell into step beside him. "This winter landscape is beautiful," he shouted into the wind, taking in the beach with a sweep of the arm.

I wasn't convinced he meant it, but I smiled anyway. Over at the landing jetty, the screech of metal could be heard from the cargo ships.

"Have you been working here long?"

"Since I left university."

His hat slipped, caught in a gust of wind.

"Can you speak up?" he asked, pressing the hat down over his ears.

All I could see of his face was a narrow band. Instead of shouting, I moved closer to him. He wanted to know what I'd studied. Korean and French literature.

"You speak French then."

"Not really."

To be honest, my French was better than my English, but I felt intimidated at the thought of speaking it with him. Luckily, he did no more than nod in agreement. I was on the verge of telling him about my father, but I held back. He didn't need to know.

"Do you know where I can find ink and paper?"

The Sokcho stationery shop was closed in January. I told him how to get to the nearest supermarket.

"Will you come with me?"

"I don't have much time . . ."

He stared at me intently.

I said I'd go with him.

We walked past an expanse of concrete. An observation tower rose up in the middle of it, pumping out the wailing of a K-pop singer. In town, restaurant owners dressed in yellow boots and green baseball caps stood in front of their fish tanks, waving their arms around to attract customers. Kerrand walked past the window displays without seeming to notice the crabs or the octopuses with their tentacles suctioned against the glass.

"What brings you to Sokcho in the dead of winter?"

"I needed peace and quiet."

"You've come to the right place," I laughed.

He didn't respond. Perhaps I bored him. But so what? His moods weren't my problem. Why should I worry about filling the silences? I was the one doing him a favor.

A mangy-looking dog came shambling toward him.

"Dogs seem to like you."

Kerrand nudged it away from him.

"It's my clothes. I've been wearing the same ones for a week. They must stink."

"I told you I do laundry."

"I didn't want you getting blood on my clothes."

If he was trying to make a joke, it was lost on me. I thought he smelled fine. A mixture of incense and ginger.

In the Lotte Mart he took hold of a pen, turned it over and over in his hand, put it down again, and then started picking up blocks of paper, ripping open the packaging and sniffing the sheets. I looked around to make sure there were no cameras. Kerrand tested the different textures. He seemed to like the roughest ones best. He scrunched up the paper, touched it to his lips and the tip of his tongue, tasted the edge of one of the sheets. He seemed satisfied and went off toward another aisle. I hid the blocks he'd torn open under some binders. When I caught up with him, he hadn't found what he was looking for. He wanted pots of ink, not cartridges. I asked the assistant and he went to fetch some from the stockroom. He came back with two bottles, one Japanese and one Korean. Kerrand didn't want the Japanese ink, it was too fast-drying, he wanted to test the Korean ink. No, that was not possible. Kerrand raised his head. He asked again. The assistant was getting irritated. I asked him in

Korean, and he eventually gave in. Kerrand took a clothbound sketchbook from his coat pocket and traced a few lines. In the end he bought the Japanese ink.

At the bus stop, there was no one but us.

"So you're French."

"From Normandy."

I nodded to show I understood.

"You've heard of it?"

"I've read Maupassant."

He turned to look at me.

"How do you picture it?"

I thought for a moment.

"Pretty. A bit melancholy."

"It's changed since Maupassant's day."

"I'm sure it has. Like Sokcho."

Kerrand didn't reply. He'd never understand what Sokcho was like. You had to be born here, live through the winters. The smells, the octopus. The isolation.

"Do you read a lot?" he asked.

"I used to, before I went to university. I used to love reading. Now it's more of a chore."

He nodded, tightened his grip on the package he was holding.

"What about you?"

"Do I read?"

"What do you do for a living?"

"I draw comics."

The word "comics' didn't sound right coming from him. It conjured up images of conventions, queuing fans. Maybe he was famous. I didn't read comic books.

"Is your story set here?"

"I don't know yet. Maybe."

"Are you on vacation?"

"There's no such thing as a vacation in my line of work."

The bus arrived. We each took a seat by the window, on either side of the aisle. The light had faded. I could see Kerrand reflected in the window, his package on his lap. He'd closed his eyes. His nose stuck out like a set square. Fine lines fanned out from his thin lips, traces of future wrinkles. He'd shaved. I cast my gaze up toward his eyes and realized that he was looking at my reflection in the glass too. That same look he'd given me when he arrived at the hotel, friendly and slightly bored at the same time. I looked down. Our stop was announced. Kerrand brushed his fingers against my shoulder as he set off down the alleyway.

"Thanks for this afternoon."

That evening he wasn't there again at dinner. Feeling emboldened after our walk, I took him a tray of food that was less spicy than the meal served to the other guests.

He was sitting on the edge of the bed, his stooping figure silhouetted against the paper wall. The door had been left ajar. Pressing my face to the doorframe, I could see his hand moving over a sheet of paper. He'd placed the paper on top of a box on his lap. The pencil between his fingers was finding its way, moving forward and backward, hesitating, searching again. The point hadn't touched the paper yet. Kerrand began to draw, with uneven strokes. He went over the lines several times, as if to erase and correct, etching the contours into the paper. The image was impossible to make out. Branches of a tree, or a heap of scrap metal perhaps. Eventually I recognized the shape of an eye. A dark eye beneath a tangle of hair. The pencil continued in its path until a female form emerged. Eyes a bit too large, a tiny mouth. She was perfect, he should have stopped there. But he carried on, going over the features, gradually twisting the lips, warping the chin, distorting the image. Then, taking a pen, he daubed ink slowly and purposefully over the paper until the woman was nothing more than a black, misshapen blob. He placed the sheet of paper on the desk.

Ink dripped down on to the floor. A spider scuttled into view and started to run up his leg, but he made no move to brush it away. He looked down at his handiwork. In an instinctive movement, he tore off a corner of the sheet and began to chew on it.

I was afraid he'd see me. I put the tray down silently, and left.

I WAS LYING on my bed, distractedly leafing through a book. Jun-oh came in. Hair glinting chocolate brown. He'd been to the hair salon.

"You could have knocked."

Park had let him in. He took off his shoes. Snow melting under the soles.

"Leave them outside."

He said he'd leave if I carried on like this. I didn't care one way or the other. If he was staying, he should put them outside. He grunted and did as I asked, and then came and sat down beside me. He asked me what I was reading. I tilted the book toward him. He moved my arm aside to pull up my sweater. My breasts tightened. His hand, ice-cold, dug into my flesh. He said nothing but I could feel him judging me, making comparisons, measuring, weighing me up. I pushed him away. Jun-oh sighed. Then he held out his phone to show me the website of a modeling agency in Gangnam. He was leaving in two days to go for an interview. He stood up, checked himself out in the mirror, said he didn't think they'd expect him to have surgery, but if they did, he was prepared to have his nose, chin, and eyes done. He turned to face me. Clinics were offering deals, by the way, I should look into it, he'd bring me some brochures for facial surgery. He examined the back of his right ear. Everyone had things they could improve, he said. Me included, especially if I was hoping to go and work in Seoul at some point. Although in the literary world, looks didn't count as much. Depending on the job you had, of course. He sat down again, one hand on my thigh. I was wearing a sweater dress, I'd taken off my tights. He ran his finger along my scar, the long, fine line that marked the time I'd fallen on a fish hook when I was little. I put my book down abruptly.

"Okay. Tell me what you want me to look like."

He laughed. Why was I acting so hostile? He thought I was just perfect. He pushed a strand of hair back behind my ear and lay down, one leg on top of mine, to kiss me. I kept my mouth closed against his tongue. Why did I always do that, he protested, we weren't going to see each other for days. I said I'd miss him, but the time would go quickly, I had lots to do at the guest house. Jun-oh got up to leave. He said I could sleep at his place the next day if I wanted to. Then he went out, slamming the door behind him.

NINE-THIRTY in the morning. I was doing the washing-up. The couple came into the kitchen wearing matching pajamas, pink for her, gray for him. She poured herself some coffee listlessly. Her bandages made her look like a panda. She pecked at a yogurt from the tip of a spoon. He had toast with persimmon jam. They sat at the table for a while, their phones in front of them, the Wi-Fi faster here than in their room. The climber had eaten at half past five and then left for the mountains. Black coffee, four slices of plain bread, a banana, cut lengthwise and spread with butter.

Through the window between the kitchen and reception I saw Kerrand as he came in. He said something to

Old Park, who shouted my name, annoyed at his own lack of English. I left the dishes in the sink, wiped my hands, waited for the fog on my glasses to clear before I went to join them. Kerrand was asking about going to the North Korean border. I explained to him that the bus could only take him as far as the vehicle checkpoint. To go to the observation point in no man's land you had to be in a private car. Kerrand wanted to rent one. Park called the rental agency. You needed an international licence. Kerrand didn't have one. But he did have a French licence. Park said he was sorry, that wouldn't work. I suggested I drive him myself. They stared at me in surprise. Park agreed, so long as the rooms were done first.

"We can go another day if you like," Kerrand said.

It was settled, we'd go on Monday. I asked Kerrand if he'd had breakfast, I'd be clearing things away soon. He wasn't hungry, he was going out for a walk.

While he was out, I went to do the cleaning in the other building. The tray was lying where I'd left it, untouched. Kerrand must have seen it, he would have had to step over it to get to reception. He could have brought it back. Thanked me at least. Why was I bothering to drive him to the border? I was giving up my time for him. I wasn't sure he deserved it.

The colors in his room were starting to glow as light filtered through the curtain. I noticed a shadow on the floor beneath the desk where the ink had dripped down. He must have tried to mop up the stain. A thin coil of smoke drifted up from an incense burner. Beside it, a pack of incense from Naksan Temple. His suitcase sat in a corner of the room. From the size of it, he'd barely be able to fit more than two or three changes of clothes. I opened it a little. Neatly folded clothes, ink, brushes wrapped in raw silk, a book. A satchel with paper inside, the pads he'd bought with me, their pages blank. I started to scrub the floor, afraid he might come back before I finished. The ink was fading but it would leave a mark. I emptied a packet of Dunkin' Donuts from the wastepaper bin along with the wrapper from a Paris Baguette cheese-cake. Before I left, I checked that I'd closed the suitcase properly.

On the landing of the main building, the couple were getting ready to go out. He had his arm round her waist, while she hung on to him, teetering bird-like on her high heels. He asked me to clean their room before they came back that afternoon. I did it quickly. Change the sheets, air the room. In their bin, two condoms, packaging from a night-time face cream, mandarin peelings.

JUN-OH WAS still asleep, lying with his back against my stomach. I ran my finger along the line of his shoulders. The alarm rang. He turned it off, moaning. His breath smelled of soju. We'd had too much to drink, my head felt heavy. My arms around him, unreal. He reached out for his Polaroid at the end of the bed and framed me in the viewfinder, he wanted an image of me to take with him. I pulled the sheet up to hide my face. He took the picture. When I looked up, he was tightening his belt. He'd lost weight, muscle. He pursed his lips in concentration as he buttoned his shirt. Like a child, I thought, feeling irritated. When he came back from the bathroom he kissed me on the forehead, picked up his bag, gave me his keys to keep until he returned from the capital, and left.

I waited for the sound of his footsteps on the stairs to die away before getting up. He'd left the photo behind, on the bed. I turned it over. The colors were still developing. Portrait view. The curve of my hips in the foreground, a wasteland of ribs and shoulder blades receding into the distance. My bones sticking out. I was surprised at how much. But I never saw myself from behind, so it made sense that I didn't recognize myself in the image. I dressed hurriedly, without taking a shower.

Jun-oh lived in a studio flat in the city center, a good distance from the guest house. I had enough time to walk back, it was still early. On the beach, snow was melting on the sand in a shaft of sunlight. I thought I saw the outline of a man hunched over in a wool coat, like a willow in the wind.

There was no one there.

IT STARTED RAINING when I got back. Park usually covered the outdoor furniture with a tarpaulin he kept on the roof terrace. I went to fetch it. The trap door was open. Kerrand, leaning against the railing, under an umbrella. He greeted me with a nod and went back to looking out at the city.

"Looks like it's made of Playmobil," he said as I began to head back down clutching the tarpaulin.

"Sorry?"

"Those little bright-colored toy characters—"

"I know what Playmobil is."

"They always come with extra pieces when you buy a box of them, little buildings with brightly colored roofs. That's what Sokcho reminds me of."

I'd never really looked closely at Sokcho. I'd never thought of it as particularly interesting. I walked over to join Kerrand. Before us, a jumble of orange and blue corrugated roofs, the burnt-out ruin of the cinema. Further off, the port and fish market. Kerrand was casting me a sidelong glance. He thanked me for doing his room. I nodded without really looking at him.

He'd paid for half-board but he never appeared for meals. Perhaps he didn't like Korean food. The evening before, I'd told him I'd make a French dish, pasta in a crème fraîche sauce. He didn't show up, the other guests didn't like the pasta, nor did Park, and I'd found pastry wrappers in his room again. I'd made up my mind to stop putting myself out for this foreigner who showed no interest in local cuisine. But his drawing was wound through my thoughts; I couldn't get it out of my head.

I stood there for a moment, not moving.

"Are we still going to the border on Monday?" he asked.

"Yes."

Feeling suddenly annoyed, I turned to face him. Was he going to stay on the roof for much longer? If not, I'd lock up. He stayed.

I decided to go to the *jjimjilbang*. I hadn't had a soak in a sulfur bath for ages, it would do me good. I scrubbed myself for a long time with a boar-bristle brush, scraping away dead skin cells and sebum from all the different parts of my body: feet, legs, backside, belly, shoulders, and breasts. Then I plunged into the scalding water until my skin dissolved into a mass of muscle and fat as pink as the scar on my thigh.

THE WIND WAS sweeping the clouds over the surface of the road. Late afternoon light. Skeletal remains of villages on either side of the road. Cardboard boxes, plastic waste, blue metal sheets. No urban sprawl. Gangwon Province had been left to rot since the war. I told Kerrand to drive faster or we'd be late for the tour. I translated the road signs for him. I'd handed him the keys as we got in the car. I hated driving, I'd never intended to drive him there. It suited him fine.

At the checkpoint, a soldier younger than me made us fill in forms. A loudspeaker was delivering instructions on a loop. No photography. No filming. No leaving the marked pathway. No loud voices. No laughing. I handed the papers back to the soldier. He saluted and the fence opened onto no man's land. Gray and beige as far as the eye could see. Reeds. Marshes. Here and there, a tree. It was two kilometers to the observation point. We had an armed convoy as our escort at first. Then it turned off and we were alone. The road started to snake between snow-filled ditches. Suddenly, Kerrand put his foot on the brake and I was thrown against the windshield.

"I thought she was going to cross," he mumbled, his hands clutching the steering wheel.

By the side of the road, a woman. Hunched beneath a pink jacket. Kerrand signaled to her to cross. She stood there, not moving, her hands crossed behind her back. He started up again carefully. I could see her in the side mirror, following us with her eyes. She watched us until we disappeared from view round a bend. My throat was feeling dry from the heater.

In the car park at the observation point, the wind whipped our coats against our legs. A smell of cold oil wafted toward us from a *tteok* stall. Kerrand buried his hands in his pockets, his sketchbook protruding from the right pocket. We climbed the hill as far as the lookout point. A line of binoculars. For five hundred won, you could gaze at North Korea. I slid a coin in the slot. It was so cold our eyelids stuck to the metal frames. To the right, the ocean. To the left, a wall of mountains. Ahead of us, fog. Not much of a view, but what could you expect in this weather? We went back down to the car park.

The old lady we'd seen earlier was there, talking to the woman selling tteok at the stall. As soon as she saw me she was all over me, talking at me and stroking my cheek with her rough hand. I pushed her away. She whimpered. I clutched at Kerrand, he calmly put his arm around my shoulders.

"What did she say?"

"We're God's children. She thinks I'm pretty."

The woman at the stall pointed to a dumpling floating in the pot. Oil was seeping from its pores, expelling little bubbles of air. I shook my head. The other woman was still whining. Kerrand drew me toward the car.

Inside, I wedged my legs against the heater, rubbed my hands between my thighs. I wasn't warming up. We headed toward the museum. It was late in the afternoon, I hadn't eaten since the evening before. A Choco Pie had burst out of its purple wrapper at the bottom of my bag and I began picking at it, one crumb at a time.

"When was the last time you were here?" asked Kerrand.

"This is my first time."

"You've never been here before? Out of a feeling of solidarity, I mean?"

"Shedding a few tears behind a pair of binoculars? You call that solidarity?"

"That's not what I meant."

"Tourists are the only ones who come here."

Kerrand didn't respond. At the museum entrance, inside a sterile box, a woman's face leaned in, mouth close to the microphone. Five thousand won.

"For two?" I asked.

A pair of bulging eyes looked languidly up at me. Yes, for two people, she said in English. I choked back the humiliation of not being addressed in my own language in front of Kerrand. A rubber-gloved hand pointed us in the right direction.

Too much of everything. Too big, too cold, too empty. The clatter of our shoes on the marble slabs rang out.

Kerrand wandered aimlessly, hands in his pockets, looking distracted. Eventually he stopped in front of a display of leather helmets and asked me to translate a sign.

It gave a summary of the conflict between the two Koreas that began in 1950, the North supported by the Soviets and China, the South by the U.S. and the United Nations, the signing of the armistice on July 27, 1953 and the creation of this frontier on the 38th parallel, the world's most heavily militarized border, in the midst of a no man's land four kilometers wide and 238 kilometers in length. In the course of those three years, two to four million deaths, both civilian and military. No peace treaty had ever been signed.

Kerrand was listening to me intently, head down, one hand on his forehead to hold back his hair. The only display that had caught my attention was one with schoolchildren's shoes from the North along with Choco Pies packaged in blue instead of their trademark purple. Were they the real thing? Did they actually have a cake inside or had they been specially made for the museum?

I checked the time on my phone. The tip of my finger had gone white. I touched it and felt nothing. Ten minutes later the blood still wasn't flowing back. I signaled to Kerrand. He held my fingers in his warm hand and said it wasn't normal for me to be so cold. I said I was always cold. He shook his head, tucked my hand into his pocket.

The last room in the museum was a reconstruction of a military camp. At the far end, wax figures of men lying on straw. The room doubled as a souvenir shop. You could purchase Pyongyang alcohol, children's drawings, badges with images of the North's dictators. Behind the counter, a waxwork of a woman in a gray uniform staring straight ahead. I walked up to it. The eyelids twitched. A real live person. Sales staff. I tried to catch her eye. No movement of the lips, no raising of the eyebrows.

I told Kerrand I wanted to go.

We drove back in silence. The rain hammered down, the sea rising beneath it in spikes like the spines of a sea urchin. Kerrand drove with his left hand on the wheel, the other on the gearstick, brushing against my knee. Between us, his sketchbook his gloves resting on it. Shadows on his nails, traces of ink. I felt uneasy and did my best to stay close to the door. The angle of the seat made my position uncomfortable.

That evening, I spied on him again through the half-open door. He looked older, bent over at his desk. He'd scribbled an image of a woman's torso, bare-breasted, her back arched, feet half-hidden beneath one buttock. Curled on a futon. He sketched a wooden floor, filled in the details of the futon, as if to avoid the faceless body clamoring for life. He finished the background in pencil and took up his pen to give her eyes. The woman sat up. Straight-backed. Hair swept back. The chin awaiting a mouth. Kerrand's breath came faster and faster, in time with the strokes of his pen, until a set of white teeth exploded into laughter on the page. The sound too deep for a woman's laugh. Kerrand knocked over the inkpot, the woman reeled, tried to cry out again, but the ink slid between her lips, blacking her out until she vanished completely.

THE KOREAN search engine had no information on "Yan Kerrand." But google.fr gave me access to pages from his books. He signed his work "Yan." The tenth and final volume of his most well-known series would be out the following year. I learned from the readers' and reviewers' comments that it was about a globe-trotting archaeologist. A different location for each book, a voyage in monochrome ink wash. No dialogue, very few words. A lone figure. With a striking resemblance to the author. Clean lines, his silhouette standing out clearly against the other mostly shadow-like figures. A lumbering giant, dwarfing all others. Or else, in miniature, only the hero's features discernible. The others, hidden behind the detail of a chair, a stone, a leaf. A publicity photo showed Kerrand receiving a prize. Smiling sheepishly. A red-haired woman at his side, almost his height, square face, short hair. A publicist? His wife? They didn't look right together. A married man wouldn't leave for a trip with no definite return date, I thought. She didn't look like the woman I'd watched him draw the other evening. That woman had softer lines.

MY ROOM WAS bathed in cold light. I opened the window. I closed it again once I was fully awake. I pulled on a jumper, changed my mind, put on a tunic dress instead. I inspected myself in the mirror. Took off the tunic. My hair was sticking up. I licked my palm to smooth it down on my head, put the jumper back on again.

The boy was in the kitchen, he looked disheveled. His girlfriend was still sleeping, he said, she wouldn't be coming down for breakfast. The Japanese man didn't appear either. I'd given up expecting to see Kerrand.

There was nothing for me to do, so I had a coffee with plenty of milk.

My phone rang. Jun-oh. He'd been gone for two days and his image was becoming a blur. He'd been held up, he was staying on in Seoul for longer than he'd planned, on a trial basis. He told me he missed me but didn't ask how I was.

Park arrived and asked me to make some red-bean *tteok*. I asked if he'd seen the climber. He muttered something about the Japanese man going back to Tokyo the evening before, I'd have known if I'd done his room.

"It was my day off," I said in my defense.

I should have done it anyway, he retorted, in case new guests arrived. As if we were swamped with bookings, I thought to myself.

Park kept one eye on me from behind the counter all morning. He must have noticed I was treating the Frenchman differently from the other guests. It was almost two weeks since Kerrand had arrived. He wasn't around much but he left his door open, even when he was out. I cleaned his room meticulously, doing my best not to disturb his belongings. Occasionally I came across sketches of his main character. Nothing definitive, he threw away a lot of paper. I'd find the woman from the night-time drawings in the wastepaper basket, ripped to shreds.

My mother had arranged for us to meet that afternoon so she could buy me a traditional outfit. Lunar New Year was coming up and she felt it was time I started dressing like a woman. That made me laugh. I hadn't worn the traditional Seollal costume for years, but my aunt, my mother's older sister, was coming to visit us from Seoul. My mother would do her best to make me look shiny.

Kerrand came walking toward me along Mother Kim's alleyway carrying his bedspread, unaware of the sheet of ice underfoot. I was about to warn him when he slipped and fell. I ran over to him.

"It's too dark." He winced as he picked himself up.

"It is winter."

"Yes."

"You get used to it."

"Do you?"

He dried himself off, his face ruddy from the cold.

"Yes, you do," I lied. I looked around us.

"The neon lights, the whole thing. You get used to it."

He rubbed his gloves together to brush off the dirt. I pointed to the bedspread on the ground.

"So you've decided to give me your laundry after all?"

He picked up the bedspread, my attempt at a joke apparently lost on him. He apologized for having spilled ink on the bedding. He seemed embarrassed, I said it didn't matter.

"Can I leave it with you?"

I held my arms out. He shook his head.

"I didn't mean for you to carry it, I just wanted to know if you could wash it."

"Yes, I told you I could."

"Shall I put it in the machine?"

"No, it needs special stuff for the ink."

His shoulders dropped.

"Leave it all in your room, I'll deal with it."

"It's in the way there. Let me put it somewhere for you."

I'd be late for my mother, but I didn't mind. If anything, I was quite pleased.

In the laundry room, I told Kerrand I'd googled him and found some of his work online. He asked me if I read comic books. Not very often. But I was interested in them.

"You have a book coming out soon, don't you?"

"So my publisher says."

"Stuck for inspiration?"

He gave a wry laugh.

"Inspiration's only a small part of it."

"Your drawings are really good."

It occurred to me that I knew nothing about art. I didn't know how pictures were supposed to be judged.

"What I mean is, I like them."

I hoped he wouldn't ask me to describe what I liked about his drawings, not in English anyway. And I hadn't spoken a word of French for two years. I daubed stain remover on the bedspread, uncomfortably aware of Kerrand's presence behind me. I hadn't used any deodorant and the heat and steam were making me sweat. Finally, he left the room. I unfolded the sheet. The shirt he'd been wearing the evening I'd watched him drawing fell out. I rubbed the fabric between my fingers, unlocking its lingering odor of incense and ginger.

MY MOTHER looked on while the shop assistant had me try on various outfits. We agreed on one in red and yellow, the colors of youth. A jacket with balloon sleeves and a silk skirt that sat underneath my breasts and covered me all the way down to my feet. I looked obese.

As we came out of the shop, my mother turned to the window display and pointed to a pink blouse with gold embroidery.

"What do you think of that for me?" she asked.

I laughed. She pursed her lips and looked down. I tried to put things right by saying I wasn't laughing at her, she should try it on, she hadn't bought herself anything new in ages. She adjusted her bag on her shoulder and said it wasn't her style anyway.

I hardly ever saw my mother without her waterproof work overalls. She had on a pair of velour trousers that day, with sensible shoes, her hair tied back with a red bandana that clashed with her lipstick. She was holding her hand to her diaphragm as she walked, her breathing labored. I gave her a worried look, she said it was nothing, just a twinge. Probably the humidity. I told her she should make an appointment to see the doctor.

"Stop fussing. Come on. Let's eat somewhere. For once I have a chance to spend some time with you."

I followed reluctantly.

We stopped at a stall near the entrance to the port and she ordered a vegetable and seafood pancake with some local makgeolli rice wine for us. When the food arrived, I tried to work out how much I'd be eating, weighing up the size of each mouthful.

"Good choice of colors," my mother was saying. "You can wear the dress again for your wedding. You'll need to watch your figure so you can still fit into it."

I started to eat, chewing faster and faster, swirling the makgeolli in my bowl with the tips of my chopsticks. Gulping down long drafts. The dense whiteness of the alcohol coating my throat as it slipped down toward my stomach. My mother was talking about the fish market, about the catch coming in late. She needed fugu for the Seollal meal in a week's time and there was nothing but octopus available. I'd stopped listening, I was eating, drinking. I'd lost all control.

My mother was the only fishmonger in Sokcho with a licence to prepare blowfish. Their organs contain lethal toxins but with the right skills, you could use the translucent flesh to create real works of art. My mother served it whenever she wanted to dazzle her guests.

I coughed. *Makgeolli* spilled onto my coat. Still talking, my mother dabbed at my coat with the paper napkin she'd used to wipe the grease from her mouth. The patch on my coat began to smell of sour milk. My mother topped up my bowl, smiling happily. I felt sick. I carried on eating and drinking, stuffing myself. It was always the same when I was with her, I couldn't stop myself. She ordered another pancake.

"You look so lovely when you eat, my girl."

Barely able to swallow, I gulped back my tears. When it was time to leave I got up and staggered awkwardly back to the guest house, my stomach distended from overeating.

IT WAS customary to celebrate Seollal with the family. Tteok soup followed by a trip to the cemetery to place rice balls on the ancestors' graves. My mother expected me to be there. I made arrangements with Park, I'd cook the tteokguk in advance, he'd only have to reheat it for himself and the girl with the bandages. And Kerrand too, should he deign to sample my cooking.

The girl had been spending all her time in her room since the boy left for Seoul. I'd find her clothes tangled up on the bed along with psychology magazines, the personality tests all dutifully completed. From time to time I'd do one myself, just to compare. Are you more of a dog or a cat? She was something in-between, I was a cat. Sometimes she'd come and watch television in the lounge, a drama series, a Hong Kong Chinese film. Another layer of dressings would be removed from her face. You still couldn't make out her features.

Sokcho was bedecked in finery in readiness for Seollal. Strings of lights were hung along the main street as far as the great steel arch, its light-blue metal structure adorned with an inflatable dolphin for the occasion. The dolphin leered, brandishing a sign that dangled from its flippers, bearing the words "Rodeo Street."

In the supermarket, I stopped in the manga and manhwa section. It wasn't very well stocked. No western books at all. I scanned the titles and eventually found one of the few manhwa novels I'd read and enjoyed. A tale of a mother and daughter in Ancient Korea. Clean lines, bright colors, a world away from Kerrand's drawings. I bought it.

Kerrand was in the visitors' lounge, leafing through the *Korea Times*. He saw me come in and closed the paper. I handed him the manhwa.

"It's in Korean, but there's not much dialogue."

He flicked through the book, running his finger along the strips like a child learning to read. He looked up after about ten pages. He was hungry. Did I want to have dinner with him? Caught off guard, I didn't know what to say. He looked at me expectantly and I offered to make us some radish soup. No, he said he'd rather go out. I was hurt. But I kept it to myself and suggested we go to one of the fish places down by the water.

STALL-OWNERS WERE stretching tarpaulin sheets in front of their stands to protect them from the wind. The customers, old men. Shouts mingling with the chilli and fermented cabbage smells of kimchi and steam from the soups. One stand serving octopus, another crab, raw fish. Kerrand was shaking his head. The noise, he said, the smells, the lack of space. He needed peace and quiet. There were no more stalls beyond the quayside, only Dunkin' Donuts. A decision was needed. In the end he picked out a stand I wasn't familiar with, away from the others, the quietest one.

Three tables, a tarpaulin rigged up overhead. Red plastic chairs. A waiter spread a bin bag over the table by way of a cloth, then brought us two glasses of hot water. We were sitting in a draft. Kerrand braced his shoulders against the cold. Did he want to go somewhere else? No, he said, this was just fine. The waiter came back with a simplified menu in English. We didn't need it, I said, I could read the Korean written on the wall. He ignored me and put the menu on the table.

"Which of your parents is French?" Kerrand asked.

I looked up at him, taken aback.

"I asked the owner of the guest house. Out of curiosity."

"What did he say?"

"What I thought he'd say. That you were French Korean. And that you spoke perfect French."

"Park doesn't know what he's talking about, he doesn't speak French."

I explained that my mother was from Sokcho. I knew nothing at all about my father except that he was working as a fishing engineer when they met. The waiter came to take our order. Grilled fish, a bottle of soju. Kerrand was watching my every move. I stared out toward the kitchen behind him, avoiding his gaze. Tiling, dirt floor, knives clattering, soup gurgling on the stove. I fiddled with my chopsticks. Kerrand drew his chair closer to the table.

"Your cut's healed nicely."

"It wasn't very deep."

I had to be careful where I put my legs to avoid touching his. The waiter came back with the soju, fish, kimchi, and potato salad. Kerrand ate a spoonful.

"Mayonnaise. American influence, even here . . ."

"Mayonnaise comes from France, not the U.S."

He looked up, amused. We ate in silence for a while. Kerrand was holding his chopsticks all wrong. I showed him how to hold them the right way. After a couple of mouthfuls, he went back to his old way of holding them. I didn't see any point in insisting. He wasn't saying anything, so I asked him how he was spending his days. Going for walks, exploring the area, looking for inspiration. Had he traveled to all the places he'd drawn for his hero? Yes, to most of them. He'd never been to Korea before.

"So I suppose the last book in the series will be set in Sokcho?"

"You already asked me that."

"That was two weeks ago. You hadn't decided then."

"Do you think Sokcho would make a good setting for a story?"

I said it would depend on the story. Kerrand leaned toward the table, as if he wanted to let me in on a secret.

"If I set it here, will you help me?"

"How?"

"Show me things."

"There's nothing to do in Sokcho."

"That can't be true."

I took a few sips of soju. My cheeks were getting warm. I was quiet for a moment and then asked him where his interest in drawing had come from. He didn't know exactly. He'd always read comic books. He spent hours copying his favorite strips when he was little, maybe that's how it began.

"Have you achieved what you hoped to do?"

"Well, I certainly never imagined I'd get to where I am now."

He turned away to extract a bone caught in his teeth. Then he asked me again. Would I agree to help him if he needed me?

"Otherwise you'll leave?"

"Is that what you want me to do?"

"No."

He smiled, satisfied. But would he let me watch him draw in return? He took a drink of his soju and said:

"If you like."

Sometimes when people say "If you like," what they mean is "I'd rather you didn't." I couldn't tell. I couldn't read his tone of voice. All I knew was that I didn't like the way he said it.

All night long the town was entombed in frost. The temperature fell to minus twenty-seven degrees, the first time it had happened in years. Curled up under the covers, I blew on my hands and rubbed them between my thighs. Outside, against the onslaught of ice, the waves struggled to resist, moving ever more slowly and heavily, cracking as they collapsed in defeat on the shoreline. I bundled myself up in my overcoat, the only way I could find sleep.

IN THE MORNING, the radiators in my room and the one the Japanese man had occupied weren't working. The water in the pipes had frozen. Park said I could use the portable heater from reception until he could get the pipes repaired. The reception had a stove he could light. I reminded him that the stove was a relic from the 1950s, it was useless. I'd already tried. Anyway, the sewage pipes were blocked up, it was impossible to breathe in my room. I suggested I move into the room next to Kerrand's. Park sighed. Nothing worked any more in this dump. There was no other option.

Mother Kim was trying to relight her cooker. Seeing me approach with my clothes and my bag of toiletries, she slumped dejectedly against the counter. We'd just have to wait. So long as it didn't last too long. Her freezer only worked every other day, it was no good for the meat. Customers were scarce enough as it was.

Kerrand was at his desk. All that separated us was a thin paper wall. He offered to help me move. No need, I'd already brought everything over.

In the bathroom, his brushes, left there to dry. A trail of ink and soap dripped from the tips, sucked toward the drain in the basin. A tumbler with his toothbrush, a tube of French toothpaste. I used some to brush my teeth. It had a nasty taste, a mixture of washing-up liquid and caramel. I smoothed out the tube so Kerrand wouldn't see I'd used it. Wet socks hanging over the back of a chair. Since the incident in the laundry room the clothes he'd been giving me to wash had all been spotless. I ran a bath, undressed. The water was too hot. I sat on the chair and waited, my glasses steamed up. I was fed up with them. I thought about it and decided I'd stop wearing them around Kerrand. They made my eyes look small. I looked like a rat.

In the bath, I had fun floating as flat as I could below the surface, keeping my whole body under water. Something would always end up poking out, a bit of my stomach, a breast, or a knee.

When I came out of the bathroom, Kerrand was waiting by the door, holding a towel. He'd taken off his jumper. His skin visible beneath the linen shirt. He glanced almost imperceptibly over my breasts beneath my nightgown, down my legs, and quickly back up again. I realized with disgust that my scar was completely exposed. He said goodnight and hurriedly shut himself in the bathroom.

In bed later, I heard the pen scratching. I pinned myself against the thin wall. A gnawing sound, irritating. Working its way under my skin. Stopping and starting. I pictured Kerrand, his fingers scurrying like spiders' legs, his eyes traveling up, scrutinizing the model, looking down at the paper again, looking back up to make sure his pen conveyed the truth of his vision, to keep her from vanishing while he traced the lines. I imagined her dressed in a single piece of fabric from her chest to the top of her thighs, leaning one arm on the wall, tilting her chin upward to say something to him, teasing him, sure of herself. And then something would spook him, again, and he'd spill the ink and make her disappear.

The pen scratches merged to become one long, slow sound, like a lullaby. Before I fell asleep, I tried to hold on to the images planted in my mind, knowing they'd be gone by the time I woke up.

WITH THE GUEST HOUSE paralyzed by the cold, there wasn't much for me to do. I washed the breakfast dishes and hung around in reception with Park. The television was on. He watched and I surreptitiously scanned the classified pages in the papers, looking for job vacancies in Sokcho. Dockyard supervisor, sailor, diver, dog walker. I went online and read synopses of Kerrand's stories, I followed his hero to Egypt, Peru, Tibet, Italy. I looked at ticket prices for flights to France and calculated how long I'd have to work at the guest house before I could leave, even though I knew I would never do it. The Japanese cat over the computer waved its paw. That same tedious grin. Hard to believe I'd found it cute at first.

A beetle hauled itself across the desk and came to a halt next to my files. It must have survived by hiding away indoors before the first frosts came. I took hold of it delicately. Its legs started waving around in the air, its antennae reaching out, almost as if it was pleading with me. I turned it over to inspect its belly. Nice. All smooth and rounded. Park told me to crush it but I didn't want to harm it. I never killed those beetles. I threw them out of the window to die outside in their own time.

I met my mother early that evening at the *jjimjilbang*. She was waiting for me in the changing room, naked, holding two cans of strawberry milk, egg mask on her hair. In the bath area, I sat on a stool and scrubbed her back, then she scrubbed mine.

"You've lost weight again. You need to eat more."

My hands began to shake. I hated it when she talked like that. You're too thin. You should eat more. Don't get too fat. It made me feel like slamming myself against the wall.

Three women were padding about, pink leeches glued to their shoulder blades. The youngest was my age, her breasts already sagging. I looked at mine. Firm, like two upturned ladles. Feeling reassured, I went to join my mother in the sulfur bath. She'd wrapped her hair in a plastic bag. Through the steam she looked like a mushroom giving off smoke. Her chest rose and fell spasmodically. I told her to make an appointment with the doctor. She waved my suggestion aside with a gesture of irritation.

"Tell me about the guest house."

I told her about the girl with the bandages.

"I've got some money saved up," my mother said. "If you want to have an operation too."

"You think I'm that ugly?"

"Don't be stupid, I'm your mother. But an operation might help you get a better job. I hear that's how it is in Seoul."

I wasn't looking for another job, I said, just to provoke her. Working in the guest house gave me a chance to meet people. There was an artist there, I liked his work. I didn't say he was French.

I didn't know how my mother had been spending her time since I'd moved out. I tried to remember what we did together when I was younger. Television. Beach. We didn't see many people. She never stopped to chat with the other mothers at the school gate when I was in primary school. It wasn't long before my classmates began asking me why I didn't have a father. As soon as I was old enough, I started taking the bus home on my own.

Back in the changing room we put on our pajamas to go into the mixed section. We lay on the ground, our heads on small wooden blocks, sipping barley porridge and peeling hard-boiled eggs. When the time came to leave, I said I couldn't go home with her. I had to get back to the guest house, I had lots to do. The truth was I couldn't stand sharing a bed with her any more. She looked upset. I found it painful to see her like that. But I'd made up my mind, I wasn't going to be swayed.

In the alleyway, Mother Kim gave me one of her meatballs. I was looking pale, she said. I imagined the meat thawing and being refrozen. In the next alleyway, I threw the meatball to a dog rooting around in the bins.

There was a note pinned to the door of my room, in French. Kerrand was asking if I'd like to go with him to the nature reserve in Seoraksan the following day. My day off. He'd remembered.

SNOW CAME CRASHING DOWN, loosened by the beginnings of a thaw, plummeting into the streams, bending the bamboo beneath its weight. A windless day. Kerrand was walking up the hill behind me, following in my footsteps. I'd lent him Park's snowshoes. He kept stopping and taking off his gloves to run his fingers over a tree trunk or an ice-covered rock. He'd listen for a moment before putting his gloves on again and carrying on up the hill, more slowly every time.

"Winter isn't very interesting," I said, beginning to lose patience. "Soon the cherry blossoms will be out and the bamboo will be green, you should see it in spring."

"I'll be gone by then."

He stopped again and looked around. "I like it this way, unadorned."

We'd reached the grotto, a small cave temple with statues of Buddha set into alcoves. Kerrand studied them closely. He wanted to know about Korean mountain myths and legends. For his character. I told him the story my mother used to tell me when I was little. The one about Tangun, son of the Lord of Heaven who was sent down to the highest mountain in Korea, where he took a she-bear for his wife and became the father of the Korean people. That mountain had symbolized the bridge linking heaven and earth ever since.

We climbed for two hours and then stopped to rest on a rock. Kerrand tightened his laces, took out his pen and notepad. He began sketching bamboo.

"Do you always carry it with you?" I asked, pointing to the sketchpad.

"Most of the time."

"For your rough drafts?"

He frowned, irritated. He didn't like that expression. It meant nothing to him. A story evolved constantly, every drawing was as important as the next.

I was starting to feel a chill. After a while I leaned over to look at his drawing.

"They look like dragonflies."

He held the drawing at arm's length to examine it.

"They do, don't they. It's a terrible drawing though. I can't use it."

"Why not? I like it."

Kerrand looked again at the sketch. He smiled. Then he walked over to the cliff edge and looked down at the valley below, its outlines blurred in the mist. Crows cawing.

"You've lived in Sokcho all your life?"

"I went to university in Seoul."

"That must have been a shock to the system."

"Not really. I lived with my aunt."

Kerrand looked blankly at me. Sokcho was crawling with people in the summer, I said, because of its beaches. Seriously, it was just like Seoul, especially since they'd filmed that drama series here with the famous actor. Fans came in their coachloads. *First Love*. Had he seen it? No, he hadn't.

"Why did you come back?"

"It's not forever. Park needed someone to work in the guest house."

"And you were the only person he could find?"

I had the feeling he was making fun of me. Yes I was, I said sharply. The truth was I could easily apply for a grant to study abroad, but I didn't mention that. Then he asked me if I intended to spend the rest of my life working at the guest house.

"I'd like to see France some day, maybe spend some time there."

"I'm sure you will."

I said yes, maybe I would. I didn't tell him I couldn't leave my mother. Kerrand looked as if he wanted to say something else, but then he changed his mind and asked why I'd wanted to study French.

"So I could speak a language my mother wouldn't understand."

He looked taken aback but made no comment. He took a mandarin out of his pocket, peeled it and offered me a segment. I was hungry. I said no thanks.

"What's it like, France?"

He couldn't sum it up. It was such a big country, everything about it was so different from here. The food was good. He liked the light in Normandy, gray and dense. If I ever visited, he'd show me his studio.

"You've never set any of your books in Normandy?"

"No."

"I'm sure there's more going on there than in Sokcho."

"Not really."

"Plenty of artists have used Normandy as a setting. Maupassant, Monet."

"How much do you know about Monet?"

"A little, not much. Our professor told us about other artists from Normandy when we were studying Maupassant."

Kerrand squinted up at the sky, contemplating the clouds. He seemed suddenly far away. We made our way slowly back down the mountain. Kerrand in front. Whenever I felt myself slipping on the snow, I held on to him.

On the beach in front of the guest house, a *haenyo* was sorting through her catch. Her diving suit steamed in the cold air. Kerrand crouched on a rock to watch, one hand on the ground to keep his balance. Waves lapped at our feet. I told Kerrand about the diver women. They came from the island of Jeju. They dived down to ten meters all year round, in all weathers, fishing for shellfish and sea cucumber.

The *haenyo* started scrubbing her mask with a sprig of seaweed in her calloused hand. I bought a bag of shellfish from her. Kerrand wanted to stay and watch but I was shivering. He followed me over to the main building. I asked him if he'd be at dinner that evening. No, he said, he wouldn't.

I made *miyeokguk*, seaweed soup, and served it with rice, cloves of garlic marinated in vinegar, acorn jelly. The girl sipped it from a teaspoon. She seemed to be enjoying it even though she could barely chew. She'd been staying in her pajamas all day since her boyfriend had left. Her bandages were thinner every day. Soon they'd be gone.

I was putting on my nightshirt when Jun-oh messaged me. He was really sorry, he wouldn't be coming back for Seollal, model school was intense but exciting. He missed me, he wanted to lick me all over, suck on my breasts, he'd call me.

I heard Kerrand come in, take off his coat, go into the bathroom. He went into his room, leaving his door ajar, and sat down at his desk. I walked over and stood by the door to watch him.

His fingers skimmed tentatively across the page. The brush stuttered, unsure of the figure's proportions. The face, especially. A woman, she didn't look Western. He probably wasn't used to drawing women, I hadn't seen many among his characters. She started to spin, her dress swinging. Skinny one moment, curvaceous the next, arms reaching out, pulling back, the twisting form taking shape beneath his brush. Every so often, Kerrand tore off a scrap of paper and chewed on it.

I lay down in bed and thought about what Jun-oh had said in his message. It had been a long time since I'd wanted to be with a man. I slid my hand between my legs, pressed gently then stopped, remembering that Kerrand was just on the other side of the wall. I moved my hand back. I was already wet. With my other hand, I grasped the back of my neck, my breasts, imagining a man kneading my flesh, filling the spaces in my body. I pressed harder, faster, until my thighs began to tremble and a groan escaped my lips as I came.

Shaking, I caught my breath, my hand still resting between my thighs. I drew it away sharply as if pulling a dressing from an open sore. Had Kerrand heard me? He must have done.

I suddenly remembered I'd forgotten to put the left-overs from dinner in the fridge. I couldn't leave them out overnight. I put my clothes on, hoping I wouldn't run into Kerrand in the hall.

All was quiet outside. The neon light over Mother Kim's stall flickered. I jumped. A bat stirred the air.

The clock in the lounge showed almost one in the morning. The girl was sitting in front of the television, pecking at the gooey part of a Choco Pie, holding it with both hands like a hamster, touching her tongue to it lightly. She looked unnaturally stiff, her gaze directed not at the screen but a little above it. She'd muted the sound.

"Everything okay?"

She signaled yes, a faint movement of the face, eyes staring into space. The string of lights in the room made her bandages glow, throwing the scars into relief. Eyelids, nose, chin. She'd really had herself carved up. I'd probably disturbed her. She left the room. The boy would be back with her for Seollal, he'd made the reservation that afternoon.

I went back to the other building, Kerrand's room was in darkness.

I'D ALREADY BEEN WAITING for an hour at the health center. In the end, I'd made an appointment for my mother myself. A nurse came to tell me the doctor was running late and my mother still needed more tests. I decided to go for a walk around the area.

I hardly ever came to this part of town. Construction work, huts, builders, cranes, sand, concrete. And the bridge where they'd filmed the famous scene from First Love, the one with the actor on the embankment. The boat they'd used was moored right in front of me. Filled with stuffed animals and bouquets of last summer's flowers. Faded, rotting, imprisoned in ice. A gust of wind rocked the boat. Mournful creaking sounds.

I walked on, past the displays of fish tanks. Two tanks stacked one on top of the other. Long-tailed fish in the lower one. In the top one, crabs piled up as if ready to be tinned. Jiggling passively in the jet-stream, too weak to gouge out their neighbors' eyes. One of them braced itself against another and managed to get to the rim of the tank, where it stayed, balanced, until a gush of water propelled it back down, and through to the tank beneath. The fish started swimming in rapid circles. The crab landed upside down, struggled in slow motion to get back on its legs and failed, piercing the ventral fin of one of the fish in the struggle, tearing it to pieces, bit by bit. Without its fin, the fish began swimming lopsidedly until it sank, crazed, to the bottom of the tank.

At the other end of the street, the hotel modeled on an Indian palace, pink and golden. Two girls in the doorway, displaying their curves. Leather shorts, ripped tights.

Oozing winter and fish, Sokcho waited.

That was Sokcho, always waiting, for tourists, boats, men, spring.

My mother was diagnosed with a chill, nothing more.

I DIDN'T TELL Park I was going to Naksan with Kerrand. He'd been there once before, at the beginning of his stay. He wanted to buy some more incense. We had two hours, I had to be back in time to make dinner. The bus drove along the coast. Kerrand was sitting next to me. I'd been avoiding him since the night I'd worried he'd heard me in bed. But now he seemed lost in the book he was reading, the one I'd seen in his suitcase. I tried to read over his shoulder.

"I really like this author," he said, looking up. "Do you know him?"

"No, will you read me some?"

He cleared his throat.

"I don't like reading aloud."

I'd already closed my eyes. He started reading, enunciating his words carefully. It was too complicated. I focused on following the inflections of his voice. He sounded different, further away, a distant echo from a body left on the other side of the world.

The temple was built into the cliffs above the beaches. The nuns were meditating, we'd have to wait. A fine rain began to fall, dampening the ground. Then, suddenly, a downpour, rain funneling down on us, falling in torrents. We took shelter under the overhanging roof. A raspy sound of chanting filtered through the walls. Echoing across the courtyard. The building was dotted with statuettes of dragons, snakes, phoenixes, tigers, tortoises. Kerrand walked around inspecting them. He stopped in front of a tortoise, knelt down and touched its shell. A nun had told me during a school trip that each animal corresponded to a different season.

"There are five of them," Kerrand counted.

"The snake is a kind of pivot point, without it the seasons can't change from one to the next. The tortoise is the guardian of winter. In spring, the dragon has to find the snake or the tortoise won't allow it to pass."

Kerrand nodded, poked his finger into the fold of the neck, studied the joint where the figure was attached to the wooden base. He stayed there, not moving, for a long time.

In the distance, up on the bluff, a pagoda in the mist, merging into the sky. We ran toward it. The rain was drumming on the ground, blurring the horizon beyond the barbed wire on the surrounding beaches. Bunkers at regular intervals, sub-machine guns protruding from openings. I pointed them out to him.

"I imagine the beaches in France are less threatening."

"I don't like the ones in the south very much. People flock to them but they never look too happy to be there. I prefer the beaches in Normandy. Colder, emptier. With their own scars from the war."

"A war that finished a long time ago."

He leaned against the railing.

"Yes, but if you dig down far enough, you'll still find bones and blood in the sand."

"Please don't make fun of us."

"I don't know what you're talking about. I'd never do that."

"What I mean is you may have had your wars, I'm sure there are scars on your beaches, but that's all in the past.

Our beaches are still waiting for the end of a war that's been going on for so long people have stopped believing it's real. They build hotels, put up neon signs, but it's all fake, we're on a knife-edge, it could all give way any moment. We're living in limbo. In a winter that never ends."

I turned back to face the temple. Kerrand came and stood by my side. My hands were shaking. I looked straight ahead.

"Last summer, a tourist from Seoul was shot by a North Korean soldier. She was swimming in the sea. She hadn't realized she'd crossed over the border."

"I'm sorry," said Kerrand. I looked down.

"But I don't know anything about your country, do I? Sokcho is my home. This is all I know."

"Sokcho and—"

He grabbed me by the waist and pulled me back. An icicle broke off above where I'd been standing and shattered on the ground. He kept his hand on my waist. The nuns opened the doors and the perfume of incense wafted out into the rain.

SEOLLAL CAME at last. I made *tteokguk* for the guest house and walked over to let Kerrand know and to tell him it was a holiday, everything would be closed. He said Park had already told him, but thanked me anyway. He'd stocked up on instant noodles from the convenience store.

"Why do you never try my cooking?" I said, smarting from another refusal.

"I don't like spicy food," he said, seeming surprised at being asked to explain himself.

"My *tteokguk* isn't spicy."

He shrugged, he'd try it next time. I forced a smile. I looked over at his desk, Kerrand stood aside to let me in.

Some of the drawings were in pencil, others in ink. Kerrand drew his character with the assurance that comes from knowing the strokes by heart, being able to manipulate the forms with closed eyes. The hero arriving in a town. I recognized the hotels in Sokcho. The frontier was a scribble of barbed wire. The cave with the Buddhas. He'd lifted them from my world and planted them in his imaginary one, in shades of gray.

"You never use color?"

"I don't see the point."

I frowned, dubious. Sokcho was so colorful. He pointed to a scene of a snowy mountaintop with the sun high overhead. A few lines showing the outlines of the rocks, that was all. The rest of the page was blank.

"What matters is the light. It shapes what you see."

Looking again, I realized I didn't see the ink. All I saw was the white space between the lines, the light absorbed by the paper, the snow bursting off the page, real enough to touch. Like a Chinese ideogram. I scanned other panels. The frames seemed to distort and blur, as though the main character was struggling to break free of their confines. Time expanded.

"How do you know when a story is done?"

Kerrand came closer to the desk.

"My character reaches a point when I know he has a life of his own. I can let him go."

The room was so small, he had to stand close to me. I could feel the heat of his body. I asked him why his hero was an archaeologist. He seemed to find this amusing.

"People must ask you that all the time."

He smiled, no they didn't. Then he started to talk about the history of comic books, the rise of European artists after the two world wars, the appearance of characters that had influenced him, Philéomon, Jonathan, Corto Maltese. Travelers. Loners.

"I would have preferred my character to be a sailor. But that was impossible, what with Corto Maltese."

I shrugged.

"I've never heard of him. I don't see why there couldn't be more than one seafaring hero."

Kerrand looked out of the window and said maybe. Basically, it was the term "hero" that was the problem. His character was simply an individual, like anyone else, having experiences we can all relate to, in search of his own story. He didn't have to be an archaeologist. He could have been anything.

"There aren't many other characters in your drawings," I said.

I hesitated.

"No women."

Kerrand looked straight at me. He sat down on the edge of the bed. I joined him, making sure I kept a good distance between us.

"Doesn't he miss having women around?"

"Yes, he does."

He laughed.

"Obviously. But it's complicated."

He walked over to the desk, ran his finger along the edge of a page distractedly, and then sat down again, lost in thought.

"Once something is drawn in ink, it's fixed. I want to be sure it's perfect."

His hand brushed mine. I thought of the times he'd taken my hand, in the kitchen, at the museum. A feeling of weariness flooded through me. Was that what a woman had to be to earn the right to appear alongside Kerrand's character? She had to be perfect?

"If I can't convey it all with a single stroke . . ." he muttered, gathering up his drawing boards.

He tore off the top sheet, threw it in the bin. Wished me a happy Seollal.

MY MOTHER HAD sent me to look for her rubber gloves in her room. I found them between the shower and the bed, in a box filled with nail polish. Bits of dried omelette were stuck to the rubber. I scratched at it. Still stuck. I had to get the egg wet to soften it up and make it come off.

In the kitchen, my mother was preparing to gut the fugu. Before I sliced the tteok, I threw some leeks into the beef stock. My glasses steamed up and I couldn't see.

"I'm going to get myself some contacts."

"You look nice in your glasses."

"The other day you were suggesting I have surgery."

"I never said that."

"Anyway, I don't need your advice."

My mother grimaced. She passed me an octopus to purée. I cut off the tentacles and dug my hand inside the head to pull out the ink sac. Beef and raw fish smells were wafting together, heavy and pungent. I pictured Kerrand at his desk. Lips pursed, hand drifting through the air before coming to land at exactly the right spot on the paper. I always had the finished dish in mind when I cooked. Appearance, taste, nutritional balance. When he drew, he gave the impression of thinking only of the movements he made with his wrist and hand, that was how the image seemed to take life, with no prior conception.

My mother delivered a blow to her wriggling fish. Pink fluid oozed from its head. She cut off the fins, peeled away the skin with one brisk movement and noticed that the pink, skinned mass was still struggling. She slit its throat. Then came the delicate part: removing the poison-laden intestines, ovaries, and liver without piercing them. I watched her work. She never gave me permission to handle fugu.

"Do you like your job?"

"Why?" she asked as she made a gash in the belly.

"I'm curious."

Holding open the abdomen with the tip of her knife, she pulled out the guts, setting the toxic organs to one side and placing them carefully in a bag before she put them in the bin. She glanced over at the counter where I was working and suddenly cried:

"The ink!"

MY AUNT WAS heavily made-up and dressed in a smart tailored suit. She laughed when she saw my mother and me in our traditional outfits. How could anyone dress like that in this day and age! Chastened, my mother forced a laugh. We set the table in the kitchen, arranging the cushions carefully on the tiled floor.

My aunt went into raptures over the fugu sashimi. She never ate it in Seoul, the chefs claiming to have a licence to prepare it were all Japanese, she didn't trust them. Twenty grams of toxic flesh was enough to asphyxiate a man, those Japanese chefs would be only too happy to kill off a few Koreans. She wrinkled her nose. But what was that grayish color in the octopus dish?

"Your niece pierced the ink sac," my mother complained. "She's not to be trusted with a knife."

She filled the bowls with *tteokguk*, poured soju into the glasses.

"That job at the guest house is making her look pale, don't you think?"

My aunt said that she'd always thought me sickly-looking. It was probably because of the air in Sokcho, she added, sweeping the dirty kitchen walls with her eyes. I concentrated on eating my soup, studying the reflection of my face in its surface. My spoon created ripples, smudging my nose, making my forehead undulate and my cheeks bleed into my chin. My aunt thought the *tteokguk* was bland. I was too intent on ladling it into my mouth to actually taste it. My mother added soy sauce to it, splashing her sister, who cried out, saying she'd paid a lot of money for the silk she was wearing. My mother turned to me, trying to avoid an argument:

"You're not saying anything. Speak to your aunt."

I said something about Kerrand.

"Him again!"

"He's French."

My mother sat up. My aunt sneered that Frenchmen were all talk, only a fool would fall for their slick charm.

"What do you know about France?" I said under my breath.

My mother said we should change the subject. We didn't know what we were talking about. And we certainly knew nothing about comics. I helped myself to more soup and fugu.

"His drawings are really good. They remind me of European impressionist art, but they're lifelike too. Full of detail."

My mother shifted on her cushion and turned to her sister who was leaning back against the wall, her belly full.

"She's going to marry Jun-oh soon."

My aunt squeezed my buttocks and thighs. I moved away before she could get to my breasts. She said it was a good thing we were getting married. She'd take charge of my outfit and makeup. She looked me in the eye. And the glasses. My mother said I was thinking about getting contact lenses, I was such a spoiled, fickle creature. My aunt disagreed, she'd always thought my glasses were hideous. As a matter of fact, why not have me operated on? Operations were cheaper now in Gangnam. She'd be happy to pay for it if my mother didn't have the money.

"It's not a question of being able to afford it," my mother said as she served me more soup. "She's lovely as she is, glasses included, she doesn't need altering."

I couldn't get the spoon from the bowl to my mouth any more. My aunt was breathing heavily, the soju taking effect, her chin gleaming. She looked at me again, asked me why I was stuffing myself. My mother panicked and told her she shouldn't make that kind of remark to me when, for once, I was eating. I tightened my fingers on the spoon. My aunt helped herself to more kimchi and chewed it, open-mouthed. Bits of pickled cabbage spurted out from between her lips and landed among the dishes, coated in a film of reddish saliva. I stared at the bits and looked up at my aunt. She gave me a dirty look and picked up the scraps of kimchi with the tips of her chopsticks. I stood up and put on my coat, told them I was heading back to the guest house. My aunt raised an eyebrow at my mother. I wasn't going to the cemetery then? My mother gave me a pleading look. Then she turned to her sister, gave a shrug of resignation, and watched me as I left.

There were no more buses at that hour. I walked with my arms wrapped around my abdomen. I'd stuffed myself again. My stomach hurt from all the food I'd crammed into it.

I tried not to make a noise when I got back, but Kerrand had left his door half open and poked his head out when I walked past. I didn't stop, and shut myself in my room. I caught sight of myself in the mirror, my hair messed up by the wind, straggling worm-like around my face, my skirt splattered with sand and mud. If only Kerrand hadn't seen me like this. Not with this misshapen body, my stomach bloated from all that soup. I wanted this image of me erased from his mind.

Sleep. I needed to sleep.

I **WOKE UP** with a dry mouth, my limbs numb. It was dark, the clock said 4 A.M. My stomach weighed heavily on me. I closed my eyes. When I opened them again it was ten o'clock. I dragged myself painfully from my bed and let some air into the room. My face felt puffy and I took some ice from the windowsill to relieve the swelling.

Old Park didn't comment when I arrived late at reception. He'd taken care of breakfast. Without looking up from his newspaper, he said the girl and her boyfriend had spent the evening in their room, he'd eaten his Seollal meal alone in front of the television, which was just as well, my overcooked *tteokguk* would have damaged the guest house's reputation. The program on television was interesting, he said, a pop song competition.

Kerrand came into the kitchen with some muffins from the convenience store. I got to work on the dishes. Tried to look busy. He ate standing up, gazing out of the window. With the light behind him, his nose made him look like a seagull in profile. I had to make an effort not to stare. Park turned on the radio. A K-pop band who were suddenly everywhere, their latest hit. Kerrand frowned.

"You can't stand it either?" I asked.

"I didn't dare say anything."

We laughed. I turned off the radio. I should have left it alone. The silence cast an icy chill. The girl's boyfriend came into the kitchen. He made himself a coffee, scratched his nose and left. I caught Kerrand watching me, taking him by surprise. He held my gaze, I looked away. He probably thought I was pathetic. Jun-oh called and I answered. I tried to sound happy to hear from him. He'd got the modeling contract. He was coming home in two days to pick up his things. Could he see me? Of course. He'd have to call me first. Let me know he was coming, not just show up.

When I hung up, Kerrand was at the table, his sketch-pad open. He leaned over, pushed back his hair, placed the tip of the pencil on the paper. One line, then another, I saw a roof emerge. A tree. A low wall. Seagulls. A building. It didn't look like the houses in Sokcho, it was all brick. He put grass around it. Lush grass, not like the grass here, burned by summer sun and winter frosts. Then a leg. Thick legs, cows' legs, then whole cows. A port in the distance, flat land, windswept valleys. He created some shadow to finish it, rubbing with the pencil lead. He tore off the sheet from the sketchbook and handed it to me. Normandy.

"Keep it," he said. "You can have it."

STRAPPED TIGHTLY into her work apron, my mother was shucking shellfish. Not speaking. Her tools were strictly off-limits to me so I stood beside her and gazed into the fish tanks. I was still on her bad side. After a while, she peeled an apple, handed it to me.

"Here. The doctor said I should eat them."

I took a bite of the apple, my attention distracted by a sudden commotion in the market. I craned my neck to get a better look. Kerrand, down the end of the row. The fishmonger women were trying to outdo one another with smiles, waving raw octopus at him. My mother saw him too. She checked to see if her stand was clean, smoothed down her hair, reapplied her lipstick. I tried to get away but it was too late, he walked over to us.

"I wasn't expecting to see you here," he said, looking pleasantly surprised.

He wanted to know if I had a free moment, he'd made progress with his story, was hoping to talk to me about it. My mother patted me on the behind.

"What's he saying?"

Humiliated, I asked Kerrand to meet me at seven in the small café opposite the market, near the tsunami shelter. My mother scrutinized him, he smiled politely back at her. After he had left, I turned to face her.

"That's him."

"What does he want from you?"

"I'm seeing him later."

"Sundays you sleep with me. Have you told him that?"

I didn't answer.

"I saw the way you were looking at him."

"It's for his work!"

My mother picked up her fishhook. She flinched and knocked over the container. The shellfish spilled out all the way to the other women's feet. They jeered openly at her. My mother flung herself to the ground, I tried to help her, she pushed me away. So I stood there until she got up and the women's gibes ceased. Then I left.

The Polaroid snapshot was still lying there in the unmade bed at Jun-oh's place. There were more, pinned to the wall. I took one down at random. Jun-oh, lifting me up by the waist. I was laughing. We were in Seoul, celebrating my graduation, just before he had followed me to Sokcho. I looked at the image and began mouthing words under my breath in French. Half a sentence. A sound came out of my mouth. I stopped it immediately. I put the photo back, gathered up my belongings. A book of quotes about cats, a sweater, a fancy suspender belt. I'd already taken most of my stuff to the guest house, the rest was at my mother's.

A milder breeze was blowing at the beach. The waves broke unevenly, hiccupping. Seagulls poked their beaks in the sand, prancing about to avoid me. Except for one with a limp. I chased after it until it flew off. I thought they looked undignified when they weren't in flight.

In the Lotte Mart, the only silicone hydrogel contact lenses with my prescription made my pupils look dilated. I bought them anyway.

Back at the guest house I did a load of laundry. Park's beige cardigan, my other sweater dress, the girl's pajamas. I had to do it by hand, the washing machine pipes had frozen and cracked. I put on a pair of thicker tights. My scar was an eyesore. I felt like putting in my lenses. The first one made my vision hazy, I'd bought the wrong strength. The second one wouldn't stick to my eye. I was late, Kerrand was probably waiting for me. Flustered, I made a face in the mirror, opened my eyes wide, started again. The lens dropped from my finger. I groped around for it. In the end I put them away in their case and set my glasses on my nose.

WE WERE the only customers in the café. Next to the radiator, to dry out our shoes. Miniature pieces of furniture were set out on the windowsill, as if in a doll's house. It was dark. Near the counter, in a refrigerated display window, two pies at fifteen thousand won, a jar of foundation containing snail serum, also at fifteen thousand won. The waitress offered us a bowl of dried calamari. I recognized her as the girl I'd seen at the *jjimjilbang*, my age with sagging breasts. She'd drawn a heart on my cappuccino in caramel. Kerrand's had a chicken.

Kerrand picked up a tentacle, turned it round in his fingers.

"When I was little," I said, "my mother used to tell me that if you ate squid and drank milk with it, you'd grow tentacles in your veins. Or worms, I don't remember."

I laughed.

"I think it was a ploy to stop me drinking milk. I can't digest it. Do you like it?"

"I prefer wine."

"You won't find much of that in Sokcho."

He didn't answer, his attention focused on the squid. I wished I hadn't said anything. My phone started to vibrate on the table. Jun-oh flashed up on the screen. I put it away in my bag.

"There don't seem to be many young people here," said Kerrand.

"They all leave."

"Aren't you bored?"

I shrugged.

"Don't you have a boyfriend?"

I hesitated and then said I didn't. Boyfriend. I never quite understood that word, nor the French version either, petit ami. Why did a lover have to be "little"?

"What about you?"

He'd been married. There was a moment of silence.

"So," I asked him, "how do things stand?"

"With my wife?"

"No, your hero."

He gave a short laugh, almost a sigh. He had some sketches, nothing final. All the other books had followed on quite naturally from one another. With this being the last book in the series, he wasn't sure how the story should develop.

"I think I'm afraid of losing it. This world, I'll have no control over it once it's finished."

"Don't you trust your readers?"

"That's not the point."

He started tugging at the tentacle.

"The story I'm creating moves away from me all the time, it tells itself in the end. So I start to dream up another one, but the one I'm working on is still there, drawing itself. I don't know how, but I have to finish it. And then when I can finally get to work on the new one, the whole process starts again."

His fingers clawed at the tentacle.

"Sometimes I think I'll never be able to convey what I really want to say."

I thought for a moment.

"Maybe it's better that way."

Kerrand looked up. I went on:

"It gives you a reason to keep on drawing. You might give up on it otherwise."

He said nothing. I moved closer to the table.

"What's this story about?"

He said he'd rather show me the drawings. I didn't insist. A woman came in with a box of red-bean noodles, a gust of wind blew the door shut. Rain was splattering on the window. Kerrand buttoned his coat.

"Is it always like this in winter?"

"This is a strange year."

The waitress placed some marinated radish on the counter and sat down next to the woman. Kerrand stared at them, then turned to me and said more light-heartedly:

"I've always wondered whether noodles came from China or Italy."

I said it was impossible to say, people had different theories depending on where they came from. Every country had its own view of history. Did I know anything about European food? he asked. I said I didn't like spaghetti. He laughed, I'd obviously never eaten the real thing. Italians were the only ones who really knew what to do with noodles.

I looked down, not knowing what to say. He stopped laughing.

"I'm sorry, that was crass of me."

"I don't get why you're in Sokcho."

"If it weren't for you, I'm not sure I'd still be here."

I froze.

"I'm joking," he said, straight-faced.

He swept the scraps of squid to one corner of the table, then helped himself to more.

"You shouldn't play with your food."

He put it down. The women at the counter were giving us furtive looks, picking at their noodles with their chopsticks without actually eating, talking in soft voices. The place smelled of fried onions.

"What are they saying?" asked Kerrand.

"Nothing really."

He nodded slowly. He suddenly struck me as being very much alone. Perhaps I'd judged him too harshly.

"This time, when you get to the end of your story, will it really be the end?" I asked him.

"Probably not. But yes, for the time being."

I took hold of a tentacle and stirred the last of the coffee in my cup. He hadn't touched his. The milk was starting to make my stomach feel bloated. I adjusted my sweater dress to hide it.

"That red dress suits you," said Kerrand.

"No, it's too big for me, it used to be my aunt's."

"I just meant the color."

We fell silent. The women had served themselves slices of pink cake that lay untouched on their plates. They'd stopped talking. Outside it was dark. You could see the market through the window. The stands like sarcophagi with their tarpaulin coverings.

"Actually," said Kerrand, "she's the only thing missing."

He was staring at a point near my shoulder.

"The woman I leave my hero with."

"You haven't found her yet?"

"It's not so easy with this cold."

I looked at him.

"It's not my fault."

"Sorry?"

"The cold," I snapped. "It's nothing to do with me."

He raised an eyebrow and said:

"How do you imagine her?"

I said I hadn't read his books.

"It doesn't matter. You have a good eye."

But what about his hero, what was his journey all about?

Kerrand leaned his elbows on the table.

"Isn't it obvious?"

"Not to me."

"He needs a story that never ends. A story that's all-encompassing. A fable. A complete, perfect fable."

"Fables aren't happy stories," I said.

"They can be."

"All the ones from Korea are sad. You should read them."

Kerrand turned to the window.

"And the woman in this fable?" I asked cautiously. "What would she need to be?"

He thought for a moment.

"A woman for all time."

A lump formed in my throat. What did he care about my opinion? Whatever I said, he'd go back to his imaginary woman and spend the evening with her. Whatever I did, he'd be far away, lost in his drawing. He might as well leave now, then, this Frenchman. Leave Sokcho, go back to his home in Normandy. I licked the last of the cream from my tentacle and stood up. I had work to do. Kerrand stared at me. Then he looked down and muttered almost inaudibly in French that he'd walk back with me.

"I'd rather be alone."

As soon as I started walking, I wished he'd insisted on coming with me. I felt like turning round and pleading with him to catch up with me. But he followed just behind me, all the way to the guest house. Beneath the arch, the leering dolphin dangled by its fin, frozen and deflated, its smile turned upside down.

JUN-OH CAME BACK two days later, arriving close to midnight. His bus was delayed by the snow. I waited for him at the guest house, in the visitors' lounge. I'd made some ginger calamari for him. He didn't touch it, he'd already had something, he was watching what he ate now. As we walked to my room I commented on the fact that he'd never asked me for my news when we spoke on the phone. And I'd never once called him, he snapped back. He was tired of this long-distance business. It was time for me to move to Seoul, his salary would be enough for both of us until I found a job. I sighed. We'd already discussed this, I couldn't abandon my mother. She could come with us then. I shook my head, she wouldn't have a job there and I didn't want her living with us. Jun-oh squeezed my hand. He couldn't say no to this job, it was a real opportunity. I cast my mind back to Seoul. All the drinking and partying, the blinding lights, the bone-shattering noise, and girls, girls everywhere, and those plastic boys, the city strutting and swaggering, rising higher and higher, and I said no, it was fine, I'd stay here. No need for him to give it up for me. He said I was being stupid. Told me how much he loved me.

In bed we didn't speak. We lay looking up at the ceiling. Eventually Jun-oh muttered something about getting the bus back to Seoul in the morning. My feet were frozen. I pressed myself close to him. He swept my hair up, searching for the nape of my neck. I whispered that there was someone in the next room. Breathing heavily, he lifted my nightshirt to lick my belly and disappeared between my thighs. I protested again and then I let him carry on. I wanted someone to desire me.

I GOT UP early to make breakfast. When I came back to my room, Jun-oh was waiting outside the bathroom, bare-chested, a towel around his waist. Kerrand slid the door open in a cloud of steam. Seeing Jun-oh, he froze for a moment, nodded to me and shut himself in his room. Jun-oh snorted with laughter, he'd never seen such a nose. I said since he was having plastic surgery anyway, why didn't he have his nose made to look like that? He stared at me, speechless. What was wrong with me? I'd changed. I kissed him on the forehead, said he was imagining things, he should hurry, the bus would leave without him.

A large box was sitting on the desk in reception. My mother had brought it for me earlier, Park said. She hadn't asked to see me. In the box, octopus *soondae*.

On my way to the kitchen to put it in the fridge, I caught sight, through the glass doors, of the girl with the bandages. She was eating honey rice cakes, sweet *tteok*. They'd been overcooked and kept stretching out in long filaments. She nibbled at one and put her phone to her ear. Her lips moved between the strips of dressings. After she hung up, she calmly took hold of the bandage, held it between two fingers and began to tug. I could see the wounds weeping as the skin was exposed. Her eyebrows hadn't grown back yet. She looked like a burn victim, the face neither a man's nor a woman's. She dug a nail into her cheek and scratched. Rooted around. Dug. Raked. Pale pink flakes crumbled into her lap, onto the tiled floor. Eventually she stopped and looked around, as if astonished. With the cloth I used to dry the dishes, she carefully gathered up the dressings and bits of skin, placed them on her plate on top of the *tteok* and put the whole thing in the bin.

I hid behind the desk in reception so she wouldn't see me as she went out.

At two o'clock, she left for Seoul.

IN THE HALO of light from the pink lamp, Park was noisily slurping his noodle soup, Edith Piaf playing on the radio. He'd asked me to cook the noodles in meat stock, he was tired of fish. The radio started to crackle. Park turned it off. He stayed there motionless by the radio and said he'd seen two more new hotels that afternoon, near the bridge. He'd have to take out a loan to finish renovating the first floor before the summer. What choice did he have? The guest house wouldn't survive otherwise.

A piece of kimchi sloshed about on the surface of my soup, flanked by a belt of grease. It made me think of the girl's scabs. I asked Park casually if he'd seen the

Frenchman. Kerrand had stayed in his room for the last three days, since Juno-oh had left, a "Do not disturb" sign on his door. He'd stopped giving me his laundry, he didn't come to the communal area to read any more. It was only in the bathroom that I felt his presence, streaks of toothpaste in the basin, the bar of soap getting smaller. The night before, I'd seen him outside the convenience store but he'd walked straight past me without saying a word. The fog was dense, but we were barely two meters apart.

Park muttered that he was going to have to go back to the dentist too. I glanced at him. His throat throbbed when he chewed, like a sickly baby bird, newly born, dying.

That evening, I called Jun-oh. I asked him how he was, then I told him I was breaking up with him. Silence. I thought he'd hung up. He asked why. I stood up, opened the curtains. Wet snow was falling. A figure hurried by, sheltering under a newspaper, then plunged into the alleyway and vanished. Eventually Jun-oh said in a faint voice that he was tired, he'd let me go, we'd talk about it again later.

I took off my jumper. I pressed myself up against the window, crushing my belly and breasts to the glass and waited until I was numb with cold. Then I went to bed.

On the other side of the wall, the hand moved slowly. A stately dance, dead leaves in the wind. No violence in the sound. Sadness. Melancholy. The woman uncoiling in the palm of his hand, winding herself around his fingers, lips brushing the paper. All night long. I tried to block out the sound, pressing at my cheeks to cover my ears. All night until the early hours, when the pen finally fell silent and I went to sleep, exhausted.

ON THE FOURTH EVENING, I gave in and knocked on his door. I heard him replace the lid on the ink bottle before he came to the door. Bare feet, rings under his eyes. Wrinkled shirt beneath his sweater. Boards and sketches piled up on his desk, a bowl of instant noodles. I shifted my weight from one foot to the other.

"The other day, that boy, it's not what you think."

Kerrand furrowed his brow, as if he was trying to recall the incident. Then he looked taken aback. I felt stupid. I asked him if he needed anything, he said thanks but no. He had to get on with his work.

"Can I see?"

"I'd rather you didn't."

I suddenly flared up, tired of keeping myself in check.

"Why not?"

"If I show you now, the story won't come together."

"You showed me that other time."

Kerrand stepped back, as if to block my view of his desk. He ran his hand over the back of his neck.

"I'm sorry."

He asked me to go, he had nothing to show me, he needed to work.

I slid the door closed.

Then I opened it again and said in a blank voice:

"He's not going to find her here, you know. Your hero I mean. There's nothing for him here. Not if he's anything like you."

Kerrand was about to make a brushstroke. He stopped in mid-gesture. A drop of ink was swelling at the tip of the brush, almost ready to fall. I thought I saw a glimmer of pain flash across his features, then the ink splashed onto the paper, flooding a section of the landscape.

I walked through the alleyway as far as the main building and into the kitchen, unwrapped the sausage from my mother and crouched on the floor, eating frantically, filling this body that stifled me, stuffing myself until I couldn't breathe, and the more I ate the more I disgusted myself, the more my lips twitched, my tongue fumbled, until I slumped to the ground, drunk on sausage, while my stomach heaved and vomited bile onto my thighs.

A green neon light came on in the corridor. Footsteps. Park came into the kitchen. Took a good look at the scene in front of him. Me, with my hair spread all over my face. He put his arms round me, patted my shoulder as if he were comforting a baby, wrapped his coat around me and, without a word, led me back to my room.

THE NEXT DAY, I worked through my chores on autopilot, all energy sapped by the turmoil in my stomach. As soon as I could escape, I shut myself in my room and lay down on the heated floor with a pillow under my hips, arms and legs spreadeagled to escape the touch of my own skin. The only thing I could bear to have on was my nightshirt, with no elastic at the waist. I stared out of the window.

Two loud knocks on my door. Kerrand. He had to go to the supermarket again. No need for me to go with him, could I just translate one word for him?

I held my breath.

It didn't matter, he said eventually, he'd manage. He paused. Then, in French, he said that I was right. He'd been too wrapped up in his hero for far too long. He'd decided to go back to France, he wouldn't waste any more of my time. He was leaving in four days.

Then he went back to his room.

I dragged myself to my bed and curled up in a ball under the covers.

He had no right to leave. To leave with his story of Sokcho. To put it on display halfway across the world. He had no right to abandon me, to leave me here, with my own story withering on the rocks.

It had nothing to do with love, or desire. He was a Frenchman, a foreigner. It was out of the question. But the way he looked at me had changed at some point. When he first arrived, he didn't see me at all. He sensed my presence, like a snake that coils its way into a dream and lies there in wait. But then I'd felt his hard, physical gaze cut into me, showing me my unfamiliar self, that other part of me, over there, on the other side of the world. I wanted more of it. I wanted to live through his ink, to bathe in it. I wanted to be the only one he saw. And all he could say was he liked the way I saw things.

That I had a good eye. Those were his words. A cold reality, devoid of emotion. He needed me to help him see.

I didn't want to be his eyes on my world. I wanted to be seen. I wanted him to see me with his own eyes. I wanted him to draw me.

That evening, while he was in the bathroom, I went back to his room. The boards were tidied away. A ball of paper, wet with spit, was lying in the waste bin. I unscrewed the ball. The paper was sticky. The woman was torn but there was a hint of an outline, enough for me to fill in what he hadn't sketched. She was sleeping, her chin resting in her open palms. Why didn't he breathe life into her, bring this haunting creature to life so I could rip her to shreds? I moved closer to the desk. Ink, gleaming in the pot. I dipped my finger in it, ran my fingertip along my forehead, nose and cheeks. Ink dripped down into my mouth. Cold. Clammy. I dipped my finger in the pot again and brushed it down my chin, along my veins to my collarbone, then I went back to my room. Ink had seeped into my eye. I screwed my eyes shut to stop the burning. When I tried to open them again, my eyelids were stuck together with ink. I had to stand in front of the mirror and pull out my eyelashes one by one until I could finally see myself again.

THREE DAYS PASSED, time moving slowly, like a ship coasting over the waves. Kerrand didn't leave his room, I only went back to my room late at night when I was sure he was asleep. Every evening I walked down to the port. The men would be getting ready to go out fishing for squid, lingering at the soup stand, adjusting their waterproofs at waist and neck to keep the wind out before heading to the jetty to climb aboard the twenty-four boats and light the bulbs strung on cables from stem to stern, lights that would lure the mollusks out at sea. Lips unspeaking, hands busy, groping blindly in the dark. I would walk out to the pagoda at the end of the jetty, skin clammy from the stench of the sea spray that left salt on the cheeks, a taste of iron on the tongue, and soon, the thousands of lights would start to twinkle and the fishermen would cast off from shore and make their way out to sea with their light traps, a slow, stately procession, the Milky Way of the seas.

ON THE MORNING of the fourth day, as I was sorting dirty clothes in the laundry room I found a pair of trousers the girl with the bandages must have forgotten. I took off my tights to try them on. My thighs were swimming in them but I couldn't do them up at the waist. I pulled them off, on the verge of tears. As I went to put my tights back on I noticed they had a run. I crouched down to find another pair in the pile of washing and saw Kerrand.

He was standing against the door holding a bag of clothes. I tugged at my sweater to hide my legs. I told him I was sorting the colors, he should leave his things with me. He put them down awkwardly as if his arms were too long for his body, and then changed his mind, no need to wash them, his bus was leaving the next morning at ten.

"I'll send you a copy of the book when it comes out."

"Don't feel you have to."

He sat down to lower himself to my height. The smell of detergent and kerosene was making me feel light-headed.

"I'd like to thank you somehow, before I leave."

I stuffed the clothes hurriedly into the machine. I stood up. I wanted to get away, but Kerrand had his hand round the back of my knee. Slowly, without looking at me, his eyes fixed to the ground, he leaned toward me until his cheek pressed against my thigh.

The clothes started to turn in the machine, heavy with water. A dull thud. Rising and falling. Heavy. Rising and falling again. Spinning, tumbling faster and faster. Swirling to form a whirlpool, a vortex smashing up against the glass door. The sound of the machine faded to silence. Not for long. A few seconds at the most. And then the sound picked up again.

"I'd like you to taste my cooking," I said.

I looked down. Kerrand was staring at the washing machine. He was already in another place. As if he'd stopped struggling and given in, too tired to go on. He stood up and murmured:

"Your cooking. Yes, of course."

Then he left, closing the door behind him.

AFTER DINNER, my mother and I went to watch television in bed. She positioned herself behind me, her legs around my hips.

"This is the first time you've come to see me on a Saturday," she said as she massaged my neck.

"Park's going to Seoul tomorrow, I'll have to stay at the guest house."

The presenter was demonstrating how to create a spray-on moustache by firing a gun that sprayed the model's faces with a mixture of hair and glue. My mother was staring intently at the screen, maybe Jun-oh would be one of the models soon, it would be hard to tell, they all looked the same on screen. Either way, she was happy, he'd be famous one day. I thought about how I'd eventually have to tell her we'd broken up. She started to rub my shoulders, lingering on my collarbones, they were too prominent, she said. The pressure of her fingers made me double over toward her feet. The skin on them was so hard, they looked like rocks.

"You should rub some cream into them."

"You're probably right."

During the break she went into the kitchen and came back with a tube of persimmon jelly. A well-known brand. A gift from my aunt. She pierced the top, her eyes shining, she'd been saving it for me. I reminded her that I didn't like the texture of jelly. My mother looked at the label, crushed. It wouldn't keep. She settled back against the headboard to taste it. On the screen, they were talking about a miracle cream for open pores. I took the jelly from her hands and began to suck. It slithered limply down my throat. My mother gave a sigh of pleasure and the television screen went back to spraying its little clones into the room.

AT DAWN, before my mother awoke, I walked to the fish market, through the unloading area. The beam from my torch lit up the octopus squirming in their tanks. Containers filled with orange cleaning solution. Acidic smell. My footsteps on the concrete, water lapping. Amplified. Distorted like sounds under water.

My mother's blowfish floated open-mouthed, as if surprised. She'd pulled out their teeth to stop them harming each other. They were fat-lipped. I chose the one I thought was the most stupid, my conscience clear. Out of the water, it started beating itself violently with its fins. I panicked and hit it too hard, smashing its head with my fingers. I wrapped it in a bag to stop the head leaking out on the way to the guest house.

The sky was tinged with pink. I put the fish in the fridge, took a long shower, slipped on my tunic dress, and tried putting my lenses in again. This time I managed to attach them to my eyes. I drew a line along my upper lids with a black pencil. My mascara had dried out, I had to soak it in warm water before I could use it. I tied my hair up in a loose bun and stepped back to examine myself in the mirror.

My features looked tired. My tunic was bunching up around the waist. I thought about changing but I'd been wearing my sweater dress all the time recently. I kept the tunic on.

In the kitchen, I realized the glass doors in reception needed cleaning, I'd have to do it before Park came back. I turned on the radio. The Japanese prime minister giving a speech about a trade deal with China. I put the fugu down on the counter, visualized my mother preparing it. I would have to do it perfectly.

THIS FISH WAS the kind with no scales or spines, but the skin felt gritty. I wiped it down, cut off the fins with scissors, picked up a knife, and lopped off the head. The cartilage was thicker than I'd expected. I tried again, using a heavier knife. A sharp crack. I made an incision in the skin, pulled it back in a single movement along the curve of the abdomen, plunged the blade into the flesh and exposed the viscera. Like cutting into a ripe persimmon. No ovaries, a male fish. I scraped away the blood with a teaspoon, and using my fingers to avoid piercing the organs, pulled out the intestines, heart and stomach. They slid out, lubricated by mucus. Delicately, I freed the liver and severed the link attaching it to the gall bladder. It was small. Pink custard. I jiggled it in the palm of my hand. Then I wrapped it in a sealed bag and threw it in the trash.

The fish looked like a deflated balloon. I washed my hands, rinsed the fish, cut it into sections. Fillets, white and fragile as vapor. I dabbed them with a clean napkin to make sure there were no traces of blood and began to slice them up. I used the finest blade I had. The tip vibrated slightly.

An hour later, I was done.

I grated some radish, prepared the dressing of rice vinegar and soy sauce, and selected a large ceramic platter. Mother-of-pearl inlay, cranes flying. I arranged the pieces of fugu on it. So delicate and feathery, they seemed scarcely more substantial than air. You could see the mother-of-pearl inlay through them. I'd have liked to show it to my mother.

IN MOTHER KIM's alleyway a kitten ran toward me. Holding the platter in one hand, I leaned down to stroke the top of its head. It was purring hard, pointing its nose toward my fish. Eyes glazed over. The creature followed me for a few meters, mewling.

THE COURTYARD DOOR was open. I stopped. Two fine lines in the snow ran across the courtyard. Footprints leading from Kerrand's room, past the fountain, the chestnut tree, as far as the courtyard door then disappearing into the distance.

Two lines. His footprints in the snow.

I stared at them.

Then I walked along the covered walkway to his room.

THE CURTAINS were drawn. The quilt carefully folded on the bed. The smell of his breath still permeated the room. Incense. In the mirror, a beam of light, particles of dust floating down from the ceiling in slow motion and settling on the desk.

His frayed canvas sketchbook on the desk.

I put the platter down on the ground, walked over to the window.

How strange. I'd never noticed there was so much dust on the windowsill. I sat down on the bed. Carefully. Trying not to wrinkle the sheets. I listened. Buzzing in my ears. Softer and softer. The light was dimming too, blurring the contours of the room. I looked at the fish. The ink stain at the foot of the bed. In time that too would fade.

Then I picked up the sketchbook, opened it.

HIS HERO and a bird. A heron. Standing on the shore together, gazing at the sea, in winter. Behind them the mountain, beneath its carapace of snow. Keeping watch. The frames were huge, blown up. No words. The bird seemed old, one-legged, silver feathered, a thing of beauty. Water spurted from its beak, a river, the river feeding into the ocean.

I turned the pages.

People walking, ageless and faceless, leaving traces of color behind them, faint imprints in the wet sand. Shades of yellow and blue haphazardly blended, as if by a hand discovering its power. One after another in the wind, they trod slowly out of the frames, the sea spreading beyond the beach, spilling over into the sky, an image with no lines, only the edges of the page to frame it. A place, but not a place. A place taking shape in the moment of conception and then dissolving. A threshold, a passage, where the falling snow joins the spray, where snowflakes divide to evaporate or meet the sea.

I turned more pages.

The story was fading. Fading, slipping through my fingers, adrift beneath my gaze. The bird's eyes were closed. Only blue now on the paper. Pages of azure ink. And the man on the waves, feeling his way through the winter, slipping passively beneath the waves, an afterimage in his wake, a woman's shoulder, belly, breast, the small of her back, the lines tapering to become a mere stroke of the pen, a thread of ink on the thigh, and on the thigh a long, fine

scar

carved with a brush

on the scales of a fish.

Elisa Shua Dusapin was born in France in 1992 and raised in Paris, Seoul, and Switzerland. *Winter in Sokcho* is her first novel. It was awarded the Prix Robert Walser and the Prix Régine-Deforges and has been translated into six languages.

Aneesa Abbas Higgins translates from French. Her translations include *What Became of the White Savage* by François Garde and *A Girl Called Eel* by Ali Zamir, both of which received PEN Translates awards, and *Seven Stones* by Vénus Khoury-Ghata, which was shortlisted for the 2018 Scott Moncrieff Prize.